ANNA EITHER WAY

LISA CERASOLI

Illustrations by Rosabel Rosalind Kurth

STORY MERCHANT BOOKS • LOS ANGELES • 2018

Anna Either Way

ISBN-13: 978-1-7323411-7-3

Story Merchant Books
400 S. Burnside Avenue, #11B
Los Angeles, CA 90036

www.529books.com
Cover Design: Claire Moore
Interior Design: Lauren Michelle

For Jazz

I see you. I hear you. I feel you. I love you. I'm sorry.

ANNA EITHER WAY

1

SEPTEMBER

The shiniest star in the sky—that was my grandma. This worked out really well for me because when I'd get lonely, I could just look up and find her real easy.

I know what you're thinking. You're thinking that a person cannot be a star if they're still a person. That's not all the way true. If a person decides they want to go to heaven—and my grandma for sure got into heaven—then they can turn into a star if they want.

That all happened back when I was five-and-a-half.

I almost got to see her go to heaven. Almost. I was on my way to school. My grandma was in her bed. She was really sick, but she was at our house 'cause we're Italian on my mom's side and that's what Italians do. Don't ask me what that means; it's just what my mom said—that some families take care of each other like people used to in the olden days. I guess Italians don't believe in hospitals or something. Well, it looked like my grandma was staring right at me when I said goodbye to her, but maybe she was staring at an angel, 'cause my mom also said that as soon I went out the door, Grandma decided to go to heaven. Maybe an angel was standing behind me, and she was waiting for me to say goodbye so she could take Grandma to heaven. I bet that's what happened, 'cause angels are real nice like that. They're the kind of people—*the kind of angels*—who would wait for a kid to say goodbye before taking their grandma to heaven forever. That must be what happened.

My mom had been crying for a while, since that angel took Grandma. I don't remember her ever crying before then, and I can't remember her not crying since.

Dad was used to it—Mom crying. He said he barely noticed anymore. I noticed. Mom said I never caused the crying, but I wasn't so sure about that. A kid thinks about those things, you know. Dad told me one time: "Death and holidays do that to people. You'll get used to it, too."

What?!

Holidays make people cry? I didn't know what to do about the "death" situation, but if holidays make people cry, we should just get rid of 'em. Then there wouldn't be as many people crying. Because isn't that the point of life, to make sure no one is crying? Except, once I thought about it some more, getting rid of holidays would mean fewer presents and less candy. And that's no good. (I know, I know, spoken like a true kid.)

I have gotten used to Mom crying. Turns out Dad was right about that. Even the dogs have gotten used to it. But that didn't make it a good thing.

The dogs couldn't hug her like me 'cause their arms weren't long enough, but the Little Guy would jump onto her lap whenever he noticed her crying. Then he'd make his head crooked and give her the saddest look you've ever seen. And the Big Guy would slump at her feet.

He was a bulldog and way too lazy to try and jump on Mom's lap or even make his head crooked, but you could tell he cared from the way he stared with his tongue out and one eye just a tiny bit open.

That must have been their way of hugging people. To make up for their short arms, they'd give us sad looks.

But, I'm getting off the track of the story here. So, the night I realized that my grandma was the shiniest star in the sky was way before I was "used" to Mom crying.

She was reading me a bedtime story, and her tears were making all these shiny lines down her face. One of them landed right on

my book, on the word "shopping." I will
never forget it. When I tried to get it off the
page, it left a big smear and made the paper
a little bit wrinkly.

"Why are you crying?"

"I miss Grandma. Just ignore me."

Right, like that was gonna happen. Who
watches another person cry and just ignores
them? I mean, who, besides my dad, watches
another person cry and just ignores them?
My dad had actually said that you're not
ignoring it, but that it just becomes normal
or something, and so you keep going. Even
though someone is in the room crying, you
just keep making your sandwich or watching
the Packers or practicing the hula hoop. "It'll
pass," that's what he added.

So, Mom kept up the crying and Dad
continued saying "it'll pass." And that's how

life was after my grandma went to heaven. For a little while, anyway.

Then, I started asking my mom about the crying because, hello, I'm not a robot. And that's when Mom got stuck on the phrase "just ignore me." Apparently, they both seemed to think that people could do that— ignore a person when they were crying.

Sometimes I think I was adopted.

I don't ignore kids when they're crying, not unless the teacher tells me to sit back down, and even then, she would have to tell me more than twice. This happened once in kindergarten, so I know it's true.

I wasn't gonna ignore Mom that night, even though I knew why she was crying or thought I knew why she was crying. My page got wrinkly and I wanted to be mad about that. It was my favorite book about my second favorite thing: shopping. Sometimes I wish shopping wasn't one of my favorite things, but Mom says it's genetic, like my big brown eyes, and I can't do anything about it except make lots of money when I grow up so I can do more shopping. Puppies are my first favorite thing. But, anyway, when people cry you need to focus on the crying part. I don't care if they've ruined your favorite page of your favorite book. I don't care what anybody says, even your parents.

So, I jumped up and went to the window. "Hey, Mom. Come here. Look!"

I didn't have a solid plan, but I knew where heaven was and thought maybe if we looked hard enough we could see Grandma, and that would make her happy. But, it was nighttime, and it was hard to see much of anything, so I was improving[1] as I went along. I don't think that's the word. The word I'm looking for sounds like that, though. I was making stuff up as I went along.

Mom did not want to get out of bed, but she came to the window anyway.

"Mom, look up there!"

She sighed. "I'm looking."

"Now, wave!"

Mom sighed again—it's so annoying when moms sigh—and then she waved.

It was the lamest wave ever.

"She's not gonna see you waving at her if you do it like that." Sometimes I couldn't believe Mom.

I demonstrated what a real wave looked

---

[1] improvising

like, but that didn't seem to inspire her to join in.

"Mom," I said, not knowing what I was gonna come up with next. "Mom," I said again, thinking. If someone gave me a quarter every time I said the word "mom" I'd be richer than the president. I've had a *Swear Jar* since I was three, and that's nice, especially on the weekends when Dad has the boys over for beers and poker or a sauna or some of his famous chili. But I think if I had a *Mom Jar*, I'd be making the big money.

I looked up and up and up...and then I saw it. This star broke free from all its buddies. It looked like it grew or maybe God just changed its light bulb, I don't know, but it looked different. And that's when I knew how I would get Mom to stop crying.

"Mom, do you see that star? The bright,

bright one?"

"I do. That's the North—"

"That's Grandma! You never have to be sad anymore. When you get sad, just wait for the nighttime before you think of crying and then come to this window and wave to Grandma. But, Mom—" I took a big breath 'cause this was not up for discussion. "—you have to come up with a better wave so she can see you and know that you're thinking of her." And then I waited.

I never knew when Mom was gonna believe me or rant on and on about my wild imagination. Or worse, call me a big fibbulator. That was her word for when I made stuff up, which was frequently.

Mom wiped the tears from her cheeks. Then it happened. She smiled. And then she waved like she was on top of the Fourth of

July float that went down Washington Boulevard every year. She was waving to the whole sky. And she was saying "hi" to Grandma, and I think some other people's grandmas, too.

Phew.

Then she looked at me. "How'd you get so smart?" she asked as she wiped her face one more time and smashed the last bit of tears onto her pajama bottoms.

I knew she thought I was the smartest person ever, but she had never asked me how I got that way. I just shrugged and smiled because I think that was one of those questions she already knew the answer to.

Mom had started asking me that a lot lately: "How'd you get so smart?" She'd say it whenever I got her to stop crying. I'd never heard her say it to Dad, though.

Hmm?

That got me thinking....

People like to be told they're smart.

Maybe things would be different if Dad would stop ignoring her when she was sad and ask "what's the matter?" then Mom could smile and say "how'd you get so smart?"

Maybe if they both could just do that one thing....

The solution seemed so simple.

Anyway, that was the story of how my grandma became the shiniest star in the sky. It's not the best story, but it's not the worst. It's mostly just this story that I came up with to make Mom happy for a night. And it worked. The neat thing about this medium-good story is that now when I see the shiniest star in the sky, I think of Grandma. Like right now.

There she is.

"Hi, Grandma."

But, I also think about how sometimes when you're five, you don't really know what's going on. Because I'm older now, and I'm not so sure Mom was crying that night for the reason she told me she was crying.

But I was really little back then.

• • •

I think seven is a lot older than five. And I don't mean that it's just two years older. It's maybe older by dog years. So, if you aged in dog years you'd be, let's see, you'd be 7x2 older (that's seven for each dog year times two years). That's—you have to give me a second so I can do the math on this one—fourteen. So, if you were seven in people years, but you aged in dog years for the last two years, you'd be five years old plus fourteen years old (for the two dog years). That's 14+5, which would make me nineteen! That makes so much more sense because I feel a lot older than I did two years ago. I feel at least ten years older.

Hmm?

That would mean I'd have my license.

That's interesting.

If I were nineteen years old right now, I'd have my license for sure. And I'm almost tall enough to drive. Trust me, I'm tall. And Mom has taught me already. Well, I know all about the lines on the road. If the yellow lines are dashed, you can pass. If the yellow lines are solid, you cannot pass. It's probably good I don't have my license, though.

If I did have my license, I might say I was going to Pet Shop to look at the new Chihuahuas. Then once I got there, I'd put the tiniest one inside my coat and sneak her out of the store. Then I'd drive toward the brightest star in the sky while I was holding that tiny Chihuahua tight against my heart, all warm and snuggly. That's probably what I'd do if I had my license because nothing felt right anymore, and running away with a baby Chihuahua sounded nice. Unless Dad was gone and my only option was Mom's car, which was a stick shift, then I'd be screwed.

Well, at least there was a loose plan in place because here's the scoop: my whole life is about to fall apart. I can just feel it.

I'm Anna, by the way.

2

OCTOBER

So, I don't know if you noticed, but my name is a palindrome. I love it! I love that it's a palindrome 'cause hardly anyone can say that. I don't actually know anyone whose name is a palindrome. I can name other words that are palindromes—madam, noon, kayak, level—'cause I'm secretly on the lookout for them all the time. The words mom and dad are palindromes, too. But they're not as cool. I like the words that have more than three letters; those are the real deal. Anna is the real deal. Dad says "real deal" all the time. It means a really good thing. Mom says "authentic." I know a lot of big words because of Mom. I know a bunch of slang (which is a word Mom taught me) because of Dad. That's one of the many differences between my mom and dad.

• • •

It was close to Halloween and I was busy making my Christmas list. If you don't make your Christmas list before Halloween, you might as well skip Christmas and go straight to Valentine's because all the good kid gifts will be gone. My list was long. I needed to make sure Mom had time to get everything, especially Number 3.

1. A boy's bicycle (cause I'm a tomboy)

2. A trip to a waterpark…IN THE WINTER

3. Baby Brother

4. 10 cans of silly string

5. A girl's indoor basketball (Dad says I need a girl one)

6. A girl's outdoor basketball

7. Four-wheeler

8. Sled (that's a slang word for snowmobile)

9. Sled (that's not a slang word; it really means sled)

10. 2 pretty dresses (Christmas concert and Spring concert)

11. A string of 100 tiny lights for my room at night

12. Hair chalk just like Sierra's

13. Disney World

14. Tickets for the rollercoasters at Family Kingdom

15. Lots of lip gloss

16. Flute or piano or trumpet or Ukulele or guitar or drums

17. Two puppies (who like to cuddle more than nibble)

18. Scooter ('cause it's way different from a bike)

19. Socks

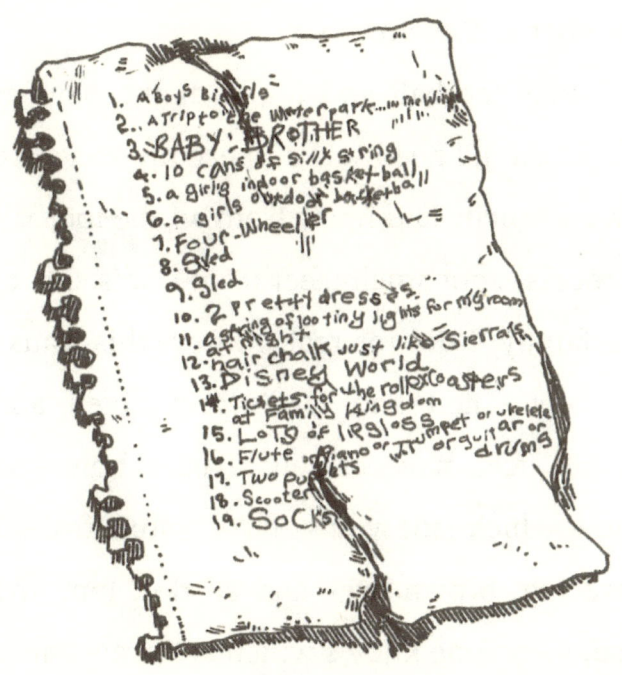

1. A boys bicicle
2. A Trip to the Water park...in the Water
3. BABY BROTHER
4. 10 cans of silk string
5. a girls indoor basketball
6. a girls outdoor basketball
7. Four Wheeler
8. Sled
9. Sled
10. 2 pretty dresses
11. a string of looting lights for my room at night
12. hair chalk Just like Sierra's
13. Disney World
14. Tickets for the rollercoasters at Family Kingdom
15. LoTS of lipsloss
16. Flute or Piano or Trumpet or guitar or ukelele or drums
17. Two puppets
18. Scooter
19. SOCKS

Number 16 was required by Mom and Number 19 was very practical, or something like that. Mom said, "I don't care what it is, but you will learn how to read music, Anna. And don't forget to be practical and put some stuff on the list that you need and don't want." I always need socks. Like I said in

Number 1, I'm a tomboy.

I play football and tag with the boys at recess. And, I need socks 'cause my socks are always smelly and holey from all the football at recess. I got smelly feet from Dad's side of the family. I did for real. I know this 'cause my feet smell and Dad's feet smell and Mom's feet never smell. That's how you know which side you got your stuff from. I have big, brown eyes and so do Mom and Dad, so no one knows which side I got those from, but my eyelashes are long like my dad's. So, he takes credit for the eyelashes and the smelly feet.

Mom was annoyed that I had 19 things on my Christmas list. She said no one is supposed to make a list with 19 things on it. She said the list should have 10 things or 15 things or 20 things, but people don't make lists that go up to 19 things. All I could think was they must, 'cause I'm a people and I made a list that's 19 things long. And I told her so.

That's when she said, "Don't be a smart *you know what*, Anna."

Be a what?! (Mom was lucky I didn't sneak up on her and put a smelly sock by her nose after that comment.)

I think it's important for the story to remember that when I made that Christmas list, my life was still sort of normal. I was glad

I'd made the list before Halloween and before I'd found out about Mom and Dad splitting, though—because I think my brain would have been too jumbled up to even get to 5 or 6 or 7 if I had waited.

On the worst night of my life, we were waiting for Dad to come home from watching sports. I guess he was taking a long time 'cause Mom was walking around and around like when she cleans, but the house was already clean and she didn't have a broom or a vacuum or anything. I was playing music on the TV and hula hooping. Mom didn't know I was paying attention to her, but I was. I could do a bunch of stuff at the same time, like Mom. It's a girl thing. We had plans and we were waiting for Dad, so we could all do the plans together.

Mom was talking on the phone, and then she wasn't, and then she was.

It sounded like the sports didn't go so well, but it was hard to hear her. Then, Dad came home and they both went away into the bedroom. It was upstairs, their bedroom, or I would have stuck my ear to the door like I did in our last house (and the one before that). I probably did it in the one before that, too, but I was real young then, like three, and I don't remember some stuff.

That's when I heard Mom start crying. Again.

Make her stop. Make her stop, Dad. You're so smart. You can do it. Make her stop. Ask her what's wrong, Dad. Tell him he's smart, Mom. Tell him. Tell him!

Then the door swung open and I could

really hear Mom crying. Then Dad ran out. Then Mom followed him.

Then Mom said, "Anna. Anna, say goodbye to your father because he's leaving for good."

And that's when I wished I could steal Dad's car and drive toward the sky with that baby Chihuahua. But it was too late.

Then Dad said swear words at Mom and she said swear words at him. And I started crying accidentally. I didn't even try it. Usually, when I start crying real loud and fast it's on purpose in order to get my way. I don't even know how my eyes did this all on their own, but they were crying very, very badly. I couldn't make them stop. It was so terrible. I ran to Dad, even though I usually go to Mom. He was the one leaving, and I had to say goodbye, and so I ran to him as he was racing out the door.

Then Dad did the worst thing ever.

He said goodbye.

Then Mom did the worst thing ever. She took me from his arms and said to get inside the house.

I ran as fast as I could to my bedroom and slammed the door way harder than I was allowed to. If they were paying attention at all, that would have been thirty minutes off my bedtime and maybe no TV the whole next day, and it was Saturday—the perfect night for a movie. Well, it used to be the perfect night for a movie ten minutes ago when I was much younger. Now it was going to end up being the worst Saturday of all the Saturdays in my life.

I fell onto my bed very dramatically, like I do when I cry on purpose. I fell right on top of my Christmas list. It ripped a little. This made me cry more. I sat up and tried to press it together, but it was ruined—ripped right through the word "bicycle." Then I remembered that I had made paper tulips with my friend, Sierra, the other day and I had glue sitting right on my dresser. We had to glue the stems and the leaves on the tulips. I was so good at making tulips. My pre-school teacher taught me a trick to making the perfect tulip. (It's not the circle trick; everyone knows that one.) You have to draw a tiny flower with three petals and then make a big flower with four petals holding onto the tiny one like a mom would their baby, as my teacher said. And make sure the petals are bloomed but not too bloomed. And that's it. I taught Sierra the other day and we made a bouquet of tulips for our moms. Well, maybe not a bouquet—they got three and we kept one each for ourselves.

I opened the bottle to glue my wish list back together and it globbed out like usual. The day just kept getting worse. Then it hit me: Number 20 was missing from my list! I grabbed the nearest crayon, which was green—not even in my top five of favorite colors, except my Packers jersey was green and that was cool—and I added Number 20 to my list:

20. DAD Come Home

There.

It was right there on my list. God had to fix this 'cause I put it on my list.

As I stared at Number 20, tears stopped falling accidentally from my eyes. I really believed this would fix it, I really did. But, I wanted to be super-duper sure. That's when I did something out of my character. That's what Mom calls it when I do something crazy, or when she does. She says we were out of our character. I looked at where the rip was, and I decided to keep going. This was not easy, but I took the whole top of the list and ripped it away. Then I crinkled it up and threw it into my closet.

The list was tiny now:

17. Two puppies (who like to cuddle more than nibble)

18. Scooter (cause it's way different from
    a bike)
19. Socks
20. DAD Come Home

But it didn't look right. I took that green
crayon and I wrote numbers over the other
numbers, so they said 1, 2, 3, and 4.

Looking at that list, I didn't think Mom
would be much happier about it. I could hear
her in my head. "A list doesn't have four

things on it, Anna. It should be 5, or 10, or 15...." Ugh. But, I gave up "Baby Brother" and "Four-wheeler" for "DAD Come Home." God would definitely understand how important this was if I turned in my future baby brother to get my dad back. He knew how bad I wished for one. Every time I saw a baby, I dreamed he was ours. I made secret wishes after I said "hi" and "coochie coo." I know He heard those. Plus, He already gave me Dad, so it's not like I was even asking for anything, not really. The way I saw it, God would have to fix everything now.

Then I got on my knees next to my bed, thinking, *This can't hurt!*

"Thank you, God, for giving me my dad back. I'm thanking you before Christmas 'cause I'm so happy that you'll make this all better and make this bad day go far away from my life forever. Thank you, God, for my dad coming back and for the two puppies. Thank you. In advance. Love, Anna."

3

NOVEMBER

My favorite thing about God was that He could work fast when He really wanted to.

Dad was only gone for two days.

He did not work fast when my grandma died. Mom said things like "what a relief!" and "at least she didn't suffer for too long!" and "it could've been so much worse." I felt awfully confused by all that.

First of all, waiting for a person to be dead who's been lying around your house for a week in a hospital bed is a long wait. (Just trust me on this; please don't test it out yourself with your own grandma.) So, picture this: I'm going to school and to basketball practice and watching my TV shows like regular—well the shows are on low, but it's all regular—except Grandma is dying in the entryway because the hospital people couldn't get the hospital bed up the stairs to her room. So, I'm supposed to do all the regular stuff I do, even say "good morning" and "good night" to my grandma who's dying in the entryway and can't even answer me because she's asleep like Snow White or one of those princesses. (My tomboy status makes it impossible for me to remember which one.) And, I did all this stuff, and I even drew her some flowers, too. Flowers are a good gift for a lot of occasions. But, that was a *very* long week.

My mom and dad had taken my grandma in after her heart surgery. They said it was to recover around family, except she never recovered and that's how she ended up in our entryway in case you were wondering. But that's a different story.

Even though that was back when I was five, I remembered thinking that God could have maybe done a little bit better with that one.

Well, He certainly did not disappoint me this time. Dad was back in two days. Dad was gone a lot on the weekends, so it felt normal to see him come back when he did. I thought everything would be normal again.

But Mom had made lots of phone calls when Dad was gone those two days. And then when Dad went away on the following weekend, she made even more calls—so many that she burned the spaghetti. Do you know how hard it is to burn something that's underwater? I'd love to tell you to try this because it doesn't take as long as watching your grandma go from your entryway to heaven, but you need a stove with the burner on high, a box of spaghetti, and you have to call thirteen relatives in a row if you want the spaghetti to turn black *and* get crispy. I think Mom's the first person to ever accomplish this. Anyway, burning the spaghetti gave me a bad feeling.

• • •

Normal didn't last long.

We did not drive home after school on Thursday. We drove to an apartment to see about living in it. It was crazy. We spent the longest hour ever talking to this guy who loved his apartment and didn't want to give it away. He kept going on and on about how great it was. It didn't look so great. It smelled. It was small. The carpeting looked like a puppy had peed on it, maybe two or three, but I didn't see any puppies to prove my theory. If I had seen the puppies, I (obviously) would have told Mom to take the place as long as we got to keep them. I think a whole bunch of puppies could make up for how weird everything was getting. (I didn't know that for a fact; it was just a hunch.)

We finally left.

On the way home, Mom said, "That guy was a little nuts. He talked more than your mom," She referred to herself as "your mom" to me a lot.

"Yup," I said because both things Mom had just said were true.

"What did you think of that place, honey?"

"Ugly."

"Yeah."

"And, smelly."

"Yup."

So, that was that conversation, well, not all of it. Mom added that she was going to find a place real close to the house we were living in now, to keep it simple and easy for me. She said not to worry because they were not getting divorced; they were only separating. I might be a kid, but even I know that when someone tells you "not to worry" it's because there's something to worry about. We drove home in silence after that. It was only two blocks worth of silence, but that's a lot for Mom and me.

"Oh, hey, Dad," I said as I walked past him toward the TV.

He was looking in the fridge. He did that a lot. "Hi, baby. Hey, how about a hug."

I turned around and went and hugged Dad like I usually did when he came home from work.

"What did you learn in school?"

"Nothing." I did learn a few things, but as a kid, it's my job to say "nothing." If I start rattling off all the things I learned in school, then it would be real tough to get out of going when I wasn't in the mood. So, I stuck with Kid Code. "Nothing," I repeated. "But, Mom and me, we looked at an apartment just now. It smelled like puppy pee. See ya, Dad!"

You should have seen the look on his face.

Mom was hanging up her coat, so I couldn't see the look on her face. They started talking like they were both Italian after that. Talking Italian is when you're loud and fast and you swing your arms around. Oh, and you can swear, too, when you're talking Italian. Mom was the only one who was Italian, and she talked Italian all the time when she was telling stories and jokes, they were all in "Italian." Dad was not Italian. I didn't even know he knew how to do it. But there they were, both talking Italian. I mean, I didn't look back to double check on the arms, but I didn't have to. I know Italian when I hear it.

My original plan had been to watch TV in the living room, but I went to their bedroom instead. They don't let me have a TV in my room. It's so lame. So, I went to their room because sometimes when a person talks Italian it's very funny, but this was not one of those times.

I couldn't focus on my favorite show with Mom and Dad fighting downstairs. I even had the volume up to 35 and I was only allowed to have it at 25. I just sat there staring at the TV, but I wasn't really paying attention. I bet I looked like how Mom looked when she was watching sports.

Ugh.

I kept thinking about things.

Ugh.

Okay, I don't want to tell anybody this— what I'm about to say—'cause it might affect my Christmas list and that thing is basically ruined already, but here goes: I knew it would be a bad thing to say what I said, that we looked at an apartment.

I don't know why I said it.

Yes, I do.

I said it 'cause I wanted it all to stop. I didn't want to look at apartments, and I didn't want to move again. We just moved into the house we were in.

One of our houses about three houses ago

wouldn't sell because the market crashed. I didn't know what that meant, but that's what they both always said. So, we kept changing houses, going into a smaller one, then a smaller one, then a smaller one, and we were renting from people. We had just moved into this last house at the beginning of the school year and it wasn't even Christmastime. I did not want to move again. I did not want another house.

I did not want Mom and Dad to *not* live

together. I wanted everything to be just like it had been the week before. It was fine. My life was normal enough, and I had an awesome Christmas list with 19 things on it. Then, bam, Mom was looking for an apartment two blocks away, and my Christmas list was down to 4 things, and Dad suddenly talked Italian, too. Plus, I was allowed to have the volume way over 30 on the TV and no one was even yelling at me about it. I wanted someone to come upstairs and yell at me for having the TV at 35 like they did the week before!

And I wanted Mom to check on me, like she always did, and say that I know the rules and that the TV is getting turned off and I can read for a while instead, like she did the week before…and the week before that…like she always did.

But I couldn't hear any footsteps on the stairs. I heard her crying, though.

All I wanted was for her to stop crying and come yell at me.

What's the matter?
How'd you get so smart?

I woke up the next day feeling all messed up and sore. Yes, I know I was just kid that was the worst age anyone could ever be—but I woke up sore. This happened to Mom when she played soccer on Wednesdays. On Thursdays, she'd say she woke up sore, and then add, "But it's a good sore."

Huh?

Whatever.

This was not a good sore.

So, Halloween happened, by the way. I bet you were wondering about that.

I didn't mess up this story, I just, well, I wasn't in the mood to bring it up, or even talk about it—Halloween. I was so mad about my new terrible life.

We went to my cousin's like usual, because they have a kid-friendly neighborhood, which was code for lots of candy. It doesn't even matter what I went as 'cause my life was so bad that dumb things like stupid Halloween no longer mattered.

But I was a ninja.

And it was awesome.

You could not even tell if I was a boy or a girl unless I turned around 'cause my hair was falling out of the back of the ninja hood. I guess you could tell, now that I think about it 'cause I spun and kicked in the air all afternoon, showing off my stunts. Mom sewed a Chinese *"Warrior"* symbol on my costume. That's what made it so special.

When my aunt saw me, she said, "Are you a good ninja?" I couldn't believe it. I looked so scary. Then she said my shirt had the Chinese symbol for *"Love"* on it, which was why she asked.

"This means *Warrior*," I explained.

She said it didn't, and I couldn't even fight back 'cause she's older. In my head I fought back, though. I told her she ought to find some Chinese lessons somewhere if she doesn't know the difference between *Love* and *Warrior*. What kind of ninja would wear *Love* on their chest?

That would be so stupid. Pardon my Italian. I shouldn't be making fun of holidays or my relatives, and I really shouldn't be calling everything stupid. I was in a real mood on Halloween. Mom would be so mad at me if she knew about this.

I was an awesome ninja.[2]

---

[2] I drew this quick for you—me as an awesome, scary ninja.

Even though my life had fallen apart, no one could tell because I was hiding under the best costume ever.

And that was the best part of all.

4

DECEMBER

Our new apartment was the size of a cracker box. That's what my aunt who didn't know Chinese said. Except this time, she was right. We had to put a bed in the living room; that's how small it was. We turned it sideways and pushed it up against the brick wall, so it didn't take up too much room. The brick wall! (Oh, you heard me.) This wall didn't have a chimney attached to it, by the way. I figured if it at least had a chimney that might explain things, but no. There was no chimney for Santa to shimmy down. I guess no surprise there considering my life. Mom told me not to give the random brick wall in the middle of the living room that didn't even have a chimney attached a second thought. She said the landlord was sweet and he'd probably let us paint it. Great. Painting a brick wall sounded about as much fun as taking a multiplications test. We also had a bed in the bedroom, but we had to have one in the living room, too, because there was only one bedroom in the cracker box. I cannot tell you how many times I had asked to put my bed in the living room back when I was young, and they both always said no.

They didn't even listen to my side of the story—about waking up and turning on the TV right away so I wouldn't miss any morning shows on the weekends. Also, I could watch TV before school on the weekdays if my bed and the TV were in the same room. And they wouldn't move a TV in my bedroom, either, which I already told you, so, why not move my bed into the living room? Another simple solution by Anna. But, no, they always said no.

And then it happened: the bed was in the living room. I remember wondering what other kinds of rules were going to go right out the window now that Mom and Dad were separated....

And then it was Christmas.

My aunt was over. Again. She was asking all sorts of questions. I was busy lining up my rock collection, favorite to least favorite, and she kept interrupting.

"What do you want for Christmas, sweetheart?"

"Socks. And three other things."

"Socks? Kids your age don't care about socks. Don't be so silly, Anna. Tell your aunt. You must have made a list. Your aunt wants to hear all about it."

She was doing what Mom does—talking about herself like she's not in the room, like she's a whole other person.

Dang, I hoped that wasn't genetic. My mom could pull it off, but my aunt sounded ridiculous.

"I just want socks and a scooter and two

puppies and…and to live with Dad again."
What can I say, she pulled it out of me.

"Oh. Well, two more dogs are a lot. Your
aunt thinks you already have enough dogs. I
bet your mom would agree. Plus, this place
is tiny."

"Anna wants puppies. Not dogs. Small,
small, tiny puppies that cuddle not nibble.
And Dad. Anna wants to live with Dad again.
It's on the list."

"Anna, why are you talking like you're
three?"

"Why-are-you-talking-like-you're-three?"
So, it's confirmed; it does sound stupid.

"Okay…. Well, maybe, if you say a prayer,
it'll all work out."

"I did that. And I thought it worked, but
it didn't. Now I'm an atheix."

"You're a what? Who taught you that word?" my aunt asked. She did not seem happy. "Anna, your aunt asked you a question."

"No one. No one taught Anna that word. Anna can learn big words all on her own. Anna has a brain, you know!"

"I don't think you should be using big words when you don't even know what they mean."

Then I got really mad, and I looked right into the eyes of my non-Chinese-speaking aunt. "I hate God. He ruined my life and didn't answer my prayer even after I cut my Christmas list down to 4 tiny things from 19 things. Now I'm an atheix, and you can't stop me!"

"Anna," Mom said. She appeared out of

nowhere, one of her many mom moves.

I didn't want to look at her, but she was my mom.

There was a tear making a shiny line down her cheek. "Apologize to your aunt."

"No. I can be an atheix if I want to!"

"Yes, you can be an *atheist* if you want. But, if you're mad at God, it means you believe in Him, just so you know. I need you to apologize to your aunt for being sassy. Apologize now."

"What? She can't be an ath—"

"It's fine. We'll talk later, sis," Mom said, cutting my aunt right off.

"Sorry, Auntie," I said.

"It's fine, sweetheart."

But it wasn't fine.

I stomped past Mom and yelled, "She

doesn't even know Chinese! She can't tell me what I can be! I hate everyone!" and I slammed the bedroom door. Mom was going to get me good now. I just knew it.

I took a couple steps back, waiting for her to bust in.

But she didn't.

Then I heard my aunt.

"Wow. What are you going to do? I know a good therapist."

What...?!

The cracker box was so small I didn't even have to put my ear to the door.

"We don't—she's fine. I'm not against that, but Anna's just mad. I'm mad. Everyone's mad. And sad. She's just expressing herself."

You tell her, Mom!

"Well, I've never heard a kid say they're an atheist before."

"She's a smart girl."

"It's disturbing. Did she learn it from you?"

"I don't know. We say our prayers every night."

"What's he doing about all this?"

"About what?"

"About this whole situation."

"The reality of the situation is—it sucks. And there's nothing anyone can do to change that."

"What's that supposed to mean?"

"It means it's happening. One day this will just be a hiccup in the timeline of our lives."

"Sounds like you need therapy. And you

need to get your [*swear word*] together. And he needs to get his [*swear word*] together. Have you filed? Has he?"

Whoa.

Can you hear a person point? 'Cause it sounds like my aunt is pointing all over the place.

"Can we talk about this later? He invited everyone over for Christmas, you know."

Yes!!

"What's that supposed to accomplish?"

"Can we—"

"It's a trap, and you're falling right into it. Have you two even thought about how this is going to effect—"

"Anna has an appointment. A checkup to go to. Can we talk later? I'll call you."

"Kicking me out. Real mature, sis."

"I'm not. We really have to go. I'll call you later. Promise."

I heard my mom and aunt walk to the door. Then it opened and shut.

I waited for a second, then I counted to nine and made my way out of our bedroom.

Mom had her coat on, so I put mine on, too. "I better not be getting a shot," I warned, and then shot her a dirty look to go along with the threat.

"We're not going to the doctor, Anna. I was just getting rid of my pain in the butt sister. That's all." Mom took off her coat, crawled on the bed and turned on the TV.

"You fibbed?"

"Yup."

I had never heard my mom tell a lie. I could not believe my ears.

I crawled up on the bed next to her and put my hand on her forehead just in case she had a temperature. She seemed fine.

Then I panicked. "Did you lie about Christmas, too? About going to Dad's?" I didn't even want the answer. I didn't want it.

"No, baby, we're going there."

Yes!!

• • •

I guess no kid should expect to get everything on their Christmas list, even if the list gets chopped down to 4 things. But I got three! Socks. Scooter. And when I woke up, Dad and Mom were in the same bed again. I was so happy I didn't even look around for puppies. It was the best Christmas ever!

My life was going to be good again!

My parents were all done separating!

I didn't have to be mad at God anymore!

And, best of all: this meant we would all be living together so I would never forget my gym shoes again! (Yes, that had become a thing.)

I hope we go back to the apartment soon. I cannot wait to pack.

I'm going to start with my rock collection....

5

JANUARY

The rocks never made it into their blue velvet carrying pouch. Instead, this was my new schedule:

Monday–Tuesday: Sleep at Dad's.
Wednesday–Thursday: Stay with Mom.
Friday–Monday: Stay with Dad.
Monday–Tuesday: Sleep at Mom's.

Wednesday–Thursday: Stay with Dad.

Friday–Monday: Be with Mom.

And I forgot my sneakers at Mom's for gym on Tuesday.

Dad said, "Good thing I'm never late like your mom or we wouldn't have time to stop."

And then I forgot my sneakers at Dad's for gym on Friday. (Yes, it was cool that at my school we had gym two days a week, but that was another story about how I went to the best school and this story is about my stupid life.)

To that, Mom said, "Aren't you glad I moved just two blocks away!"

No. No, Mom, I'm not glad. My life is here and there. I can't find my favorite mittens with the puppy faces on them.

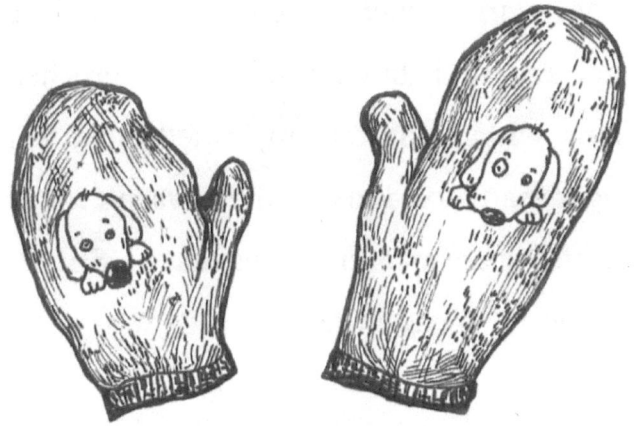

I can't remember where my tennis shoes are—ever. And sometimes Tuesday feels like Wednesday and Thursday feels like Tuesday and I can't even remember what days I have gym now, and it used to be my favorite class. I'm not glad, I'm mad! I'm so mad!

And then I forgot my shoes completely on the next Tuesday or Friday or whatever. Didn't even remember them on the way to school.

My gym teacher loaned me a pair. That's what she said, but I think they were hers. Along with being tall, my smelly feet were bigger than most kids' so there wasn't a spare pair in the box of extra shoes that fit. She said she found them in the back.

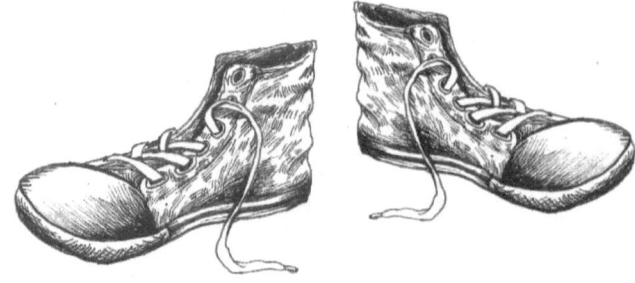

But she had her boots on. And, also, these were not normal kid sneakers. It wasn't too hard to put two and two together. Anyway, I tied them real tight—they were a little big— and said thank you.

But I was embarrassed. Not about forgetting my shoes—kids forget their gym shoes all the time. About everyone probably knowing that I couldn't remember where my shoes were because of *you know what*. Plus, no one made fun of me. Like I said, I had a nice school, but back when my life was normal, kids would've for sure laughed at my big feet in those even bigger, crazy gym shoes. A couple of my good friends would've even pointed while they were laughing. And I would've been laughing, too. But no one said anything. This is how you know what kids are thinking.

I especially knew the whole school knew about me forgetting my shoes again by lunchtime because Sierra, who wasn't even in my gym class, handed me half of her sandwich and I didn't even ask. It was from the sub shop around the corner. Special. Her mom would treat her once a month to the expensive sandwiches that looked like they were made from scratch, except they have a special sauce that's like mayonnaise but yummy. I think their secret ingredient must be sugar, but the people that work at the sub shop aren't allowed to tell. Their lips are sealed. I might get a part-time job there in high school just to find out.

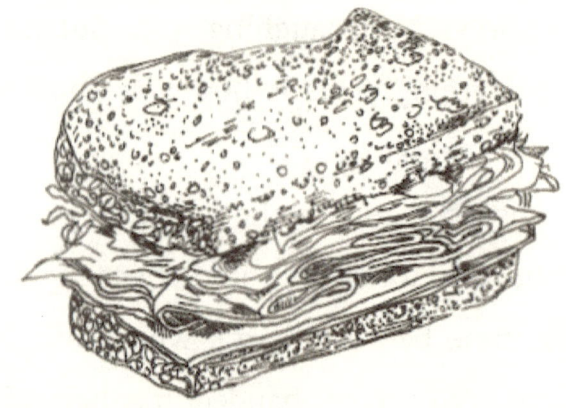

Anyway, Sierra gave me half of her amazing, incredible sandwich and then took half of my jelly and nothing sandwich (Mom was out of peanut butter). And all Sierra said when she did this was "splitzies," which was the dead giveaway.

Here was the other thing: some teachers were looking at me like the Big Guy and Little Guy looked at Mom when she cried. They would tilt their heads and smile (instead of sticking out their tongues, thank goodness), but they still looked sad, even though they were smiling.

My dad always said things like how being an adult is complicated. He said you never know what's going on with people, and that he would teach me about all that stuff when I got older.

Adults didn't seem all that complicated to me. They looked sad when they were sad, and they couldn't hide their feelings very well. I mean, they couldn't hide them any better than Sierra. They cried, too, at least Mom did. Dad got really, really quiet; that's how he was now. My teachers tilted their heads. My gym teacher gave me her own shoes and fibbed about it. Adults didn't seem that complicated to me. I could tell when they were sad, even when they were smiling, and I could tell when they were lying, especially when it came to gym shoes and tears.

What's the matter?
How'd you get so smart?

The solution seemed so simple....

• • •

Monday–Tuesday: Sleep at Dad's.

Wednesday–Thursday: Stay with Mom.

Friday–Monday: Stay with Dad.

Monday–Tuesday: Sleep at Mom's.

Wednesday–Thursday: Stay with Dad.

Friday–Monday: Be with Mom.

Monday–Tuesday....

6

FEBRUARY

What a disaster the new year turned out to be.

Thank God February was the shortest month of the year. (Yes, I believed in Him again, even though I was super-duper mad.)

All I wanted was the month of February to fly by. I wanted it done. Done. Done. Done.

If it sounds like I'm being dramatic, wait till I lay this one on you....

My mom's birthday was right on Valentine's Day.

I used to think that was cool, a birthday right on Valentine's Day. That was back when I was young and didn't have a mom with a broken heart.

About the worst thing that can happen to a person with a broken heart is to have their birthday on Valentine's Day.

I used to feel bad for my little cousin, Buggie—that's his nickname—'cause he and Jesus were born on the same day. What tough luck there. Of course, we would always get him two presents, but not everyone did that. They just pretended that the present for Christmas counted for both. (Don't get me started on how lame and cheap that is. I don't want to mention any names about who was lame and cheap but let me just say she doesn't speak Chinese.) Plus, everyone went to church on his birthday—that's worse than a Time Out! Church on your birthday?! Poor Buggie. But, now I discovered there's a worse birthday that a person could have than Jesus and Buggie's.

Mom's....

Ugh.

What was I supposed to do about my mom and her birthday?

Boy, was Dad right about the holidays making people sad.

Can a person erase February? If we can skip a day, maybe we can skip the whole month? But who would I even discuss this with? The president? My homeroom teacher? Dad? Who has the power to erase February?

Oh, right.

I put my hands together and I looked up, but then I just, I don't know, gave up.

I was starting to sigh like Mom.

Okay, so, with February still in play:

Do I get her a card? That would probably make her cry.

Do I ignore the day entirely? That would probably make her cry.

Do I not even bother to ask for Valentine's cards or treats for my class? I mean, I was the kid who couldn't remember her shoes and who people gave their favorite lunch to now. One more day of tilted heads and sad smiles wasn't going to kill me. That's what Mom would say: *"Would it kill you to use your old bike this summer? No, no it wouldn't, Anna. We'll get you a new bike next year."*

But I loved filling out Valentine's Day cards.

But I hated seeing Mom cry.

And I wasn't getting used to it.

And I couldn't just ignore it.

Looked like I had my answer: I'll just forget about it.

I was going to pretend like I couldn't remember there was a Valentine's Day this year.

• • •

I guess my mom was still my mom 'cause I came home from school the day before *the day before* Valentine's Day and there were cards on the bed for the whole class, plus a big one for my teacher. In the kitchen, there was a box of red velvet cake mix and a container of cream cheese frosting. Mom and I aren't "cake people," except red velvet cake 'cause it tastes like chocolate cake that's been run under the faucet, except in a good way. I wish I could describe it better. It's like a wet, chocolately sponge. I think I just made it worse. Just trust me, it's incredible. It tastes like dunking a cookie in a glass of milk and holding it there for ten seconds, except when you take it out of the milk, the cookie is still together.

Now I bet you believe me about how good it is.

I cracked the eggs and got bored after

that, so Mom finished baking the cupcakes while I filled out the cards. It wasn't as bad as I had imagined. Mom only cried once, and that was because I gave her the card she had purchased for my teacher. I could give my teacher a small card; I knew that would be okay. But there was no way I was going to be able to buy Mom a card on this late notice. Plus, Dad wasn't a shopper. *We have the genes for that, remember?* And I wasn't allowed to go to the store or anywhere alone. So, I gave Mom a Valentine's card and wrote Happy Birthday on it. She had already seen it 'cause she picked it out, but she was really surprised it turned out to be for her. That's the part that made her cry.

"Tears of joy," she said.

I'm glad she cleared that up 'cause all the tears had started looking the same to me.

7

MARCH

We spent spring break down with my grandparents, *my dad's parents.*

That might sound crazy, "given the reality of the situation," but that's what we always did for my whole life. And we weren't going to do it this year, but then they said, "Come, it'll be good for Anna. We'd love to have you both!" They said my mom was still family no matter what. To that, Dad replied that liberals have their upside, then Mom shook her head and he laughed. I didn't know what they were talking about, but it felt like old times, like normal for Dad to make a joke that Mom didn't think was funny and then watch Dad laugh at his own joke and make everything all better. That wasn't as cool as finding them in the same bedroom on Christmas morning, but seeing them both smile at the same time gave me hope.

…And so did going to his parents' house for spring break. It was normal, like back when I was a little kid. It was so great, and it gave me hope, too. Maybe my dad's parents would talk some sense into my parents! Well, my mom. They enjoyed giving out advice. Grandma would say: "It's one of the few things in life that's free!"

Dad barely ever joined us for vacations. He always said we couldn't all afford to go and told us girls have fun. He always added that: "You girls have fun!" Then he'd give me forty bucks. Woohoo, which he did this time, too. After he and mom shared their smiles with each other, he took out his wallet and handed me some money, except this time it was five twenties—a hundred bucks! (Because of *you know what*.)

But still…a hundred bucks!

• • •

Mom and I swam in the pool; played Connect Four nonstop; put on makeup for no reason. We went to the mall. A lot. We got nice tans, but not too much. We looked like natural beauties. Coppertone beauties, that's what Grandpa said. Grandma said Mom looked tired. She always had a hard time giving out compliments to her daughter-in-law. Mom told me that. It was probably one of those things I wasn't supposed to know. That list was getting big.

Back when we were on the plane before we got to my grandparents, Mom said she didn't want too much alone time with Grandma. Last year, Grandma went on and on about Mom looking skinny. Mom said she'd find a new thing to complain about this year. Then she added, "Let's be best buddies, Anna, partners in crime, a crime-fighting duo, so Grandma doesn't harass me about all the things that are wrong with our lives."

I said "okay" to all that, but I knew what she was up to and I was mostly thinking, *Find yourself another Robin, Batman. You and Dad said this was not my fault about a thousand times since Halloween.*

And I was finally believing them.

That this was not my fault. (I think.)

And I didn't want to fight crime or fight with Grandma and Grandpa as Mom's sidekick.

Grandma was the nicest to Mom she had ever been. Even when she complained about Mom being tired, it came out nice. I swear.

Except after Grandma's comment, I said, "She's just stressed!"

Then Grandma shot Mom a dirty, dirty look.

Then Mom said, "She doesn't even know

what it means. She just heard me saying it."

Then Grandma turned to me. "Anna, what does it mean?"

"I don't know," I said. That seemed like the best answer based on the situation.

"See?"

"That doesn't make it okay," Grandma said. "What else does she hear you say? She's got ears, you know. That's what I keep telling my son. And you're our daughter, too. We love you, we love you both. But your daughter sees and hears everything you do and say. You both need to understand that this isn't about you at this point. This is about her. And the girl's got ears!"

"Yes, I know. She's using them right now," my mom said and bulged her eyes at Grandma.

*But other than that little hiccup...*Mom didn't cry once the whole week. She said it was the sun.

Grandma said I looked skinny this year. She said I looked all stretched out, and it didn't hurt my feelings. Even though this was the worst year of my life and I was the worst age anyone could ever be, I had grown three inches since the beginning of the school year. Even after living on leftovers and all the candy I wanted, I was still growing. I tucked that piece of information away for when things got back to normal next year. I secretly couldn't wait for the day when Mom and Dad were back together, and then, after that, I couldn't wait for the day they told me I had to eat all my broccoli if I wanted to grow tall, get muscles, and be smart. I had my comeback all set:

"Oh, really? Well, do you remember the year you guys got separated and I lived off Mac & Cheese, grilled cheese, cheesy tortillas, gummy bears, Swedish Fish, string cheese, chocolate covered gummy bears—*you haven't lived till you've had those*—and freezy pops? I grew just fine. Three inches! You've both been fibbing all along and I'm never eating broccoli again."

I had the whole speech planned out. And I dreamed, every day, of announcing it to both of them when they were back together, and my life was good.

"I'm never eating broccoli again. So there!"

Grandma and Grandpa took me to Family

Kingdom on the last day of vacation. I wanted Mom to join, but they said she needed a break. She had thrown up the fajitas or taquitos or something from the night before. I didn't know what it was, exactly, 'cause I didn't get to go out for dinner. It was just her and Grandma, which seemed kind of spooky to me, but, also kind of funny. *Give it to her, Grandma!*

Anyway, they said the last thing Mom needed was an amusement park. She was ready to go, though—all dressed up in a new sundress we had just purchased from Old Navy. We love that place. There's something for everyone at Old Navy and the price was always right. It was yellow. Not a lot of people can wear yellow. That's what Grandma said. I guess it was another compliment for Mom—like when she called her skinny—'cause the whole dress was yellow and she looked prettier than I had seen her all year, especially after yakking, which was so gross. But, dang, was she pretty. I was happy she was so pretty. She'd been so sad all year—and feeling pretty, well, it helps a little. But, I was not happy about her not coming to go on the rollercoasters. She said I'd have to go on the rides with Grandpa. I loved him; he just didn't look too excited about rollercoastering, even after I told him I'd sit closest to the door (you know, in case it swung open while we were looping).

Nonetheless, Grandpa tilted his head and smiled when he said, "It'll be fun!"

Now, that is love.

• • •

Mom drove me straight to Dad's from the airport. He missed me bunches or so he said (or so she said he said). We walked in and that's when I realized, I missed him, too.

It was the first time I had ever really missed my dad.

It's different with dads. They're not supposed to be home every day or read to you every night or take you shopping or to church. And they're not the ones that make you take a shower. They do make you brush your teeth as much as moms, though.

Anyway, I didn't know I was going to miss him when they got separated. I was more worried about being away from Mom. I would never tell my dad that, though, 'cause

I bet it would hurt his feelings and I already made that mistake once with the whole apartment thing.... (Here's a piece of information I'm going to give you for the future of your life: There is almost nothing worse than seeing your dad sad.)

But, I was excited *for real* to see him after our vacation. It was a fun, new feeling. And, I had so much to tell him about the rollercoasters and everything.

I ran into his arms. He gave the greatest hugs and that one, right then, was the best ever.

I got him a bag of seashells from Myrtle Beach to add to his collection. They were in a bag in my hand and I was about to talk about them when his hug stopped.

He stood straight up, making himself extra tall. "You look good," he said to Mom.

That was the first really nice thing he'd said all year. They shared those smiles before we left on vacation and now this. I felt double happy.

"You look really good," he said again.

I caught a glimpse of Mom's smile the first time he said it. And then I watched it disappear when he said it a second time.

"What's that all about?" he asked.

Mom looked sad again. The tan had made her so pretty. And her sad look had been gone for the whole vacation—except for the day of the hiccup with Grandma—and now it was right back on her face.

"She's got a tan," I said. "Me, too. Grandpa said we're natural beauties now. We have Coppertone glows!"

"He did, did he? Is that what he said?" Dad responded to me, even though he was still staring at Mom.

"We go to your parents every year. And every year I come back and look like this and you've never noticed before."

"Yes, he does. He said we were pretty last year. I remember."

"Don't defend him, Anna."

"Well, maybe you look different this

year," my dad said.

"It's the yellow dress. You've never seen her in yellow. Not a lot of people can pull it off, you know." She had it on again 'cause it looked that pretty.

"Don't make excuses for her, Anna."

"I got you some shells to add to your collection, Dad."

No one said anything to that.

It was a stare down—like the ones I have with Sierra when there's only one pink freezy pop left. Except it didn't look like anybody was going to blink.

I grabbed the bottom of the bag and flipped it. "I said I got shells!" They dumped out on the tile floor. It was noisy and distracting and the Big Guy and the Little Guy dove in, sniffing the shells like crazy. I started grabbing up my faves and stuffing them back in the bag in case the dogs got any wise ideas.

Then Mom added, "Sometimes the sun is all a person—" but before she could finish, Dad stepped close to her and grabbed her phone off the counter. It was next to her purse and keys.

"Hey!" she said.

This did not feel good anymore. This was bad.

Mom kept looking at me from the corner of her eye. Dad kept staring at her like he forgot I was there.

Then Dad said, "Baby, go to your room." I guess he remembered I was there.

"But I have shells. I named them and everything."

Mom put her hand out in front of Dad. I have never seen Mom so frozen like a statue before this. She is a naturally wiggly person. Standing that still like she was doing—that had to be so hard for her.

Dad was starting to look like he had a tan, too…the kind that starts out red but turns a good color the next day. He finally put the phone in the palm of Mom's hand.

That's when Mom said, "You don't even know what you're talking about."

I thought that was weird. Dad hadn't said a word.

"I don't, do I?" Dad replied.

"No, you don't," Mom said back.

This wasn't Italian, but it was some kind of crazy language. I'm seven, not an idiot.

Then Mom turned to me, "Hey,

sweetheart, give your mom a hug."

I started crying. I didn't know why. I fell into her arms. "Can I go home with you? Please? Please?" I was whispering but not doing it too well.

"No, sweetheart, your daddy misses you. He misses you so much. I bet he has a special day planned."

"No, he doesn't," I said, holding her tight. "He doesn't even care about my shells."

"I love your shells, baby." Dad bent down and started picking up the rest of them, one by one. "This one looks like a Maddy. I bet this one's name is Sawyer."

"No, Dad, that's stupid—"

"Don't say stupid, sweetheart," Mom said.

"Sorry. They have shell names, Dad, not

people names. That one is Sandy and the blue one is Dolphin."

"That makes sense."

"That really big one is—"

"Bob?" he asked.

"What? No, it's not Bob. Who would name a seashell Bob?"

Dad stared at me like he was trying to think of an answer, even though I was asking one of those questions that Mom liked to ask. They're called rhetorical questions in case you were wondering. Those are questions that you don't need the answer to because you already know it.

"His name is Moby."

"Of course, it is. That makes sense, baby. I love your shells. Prettier than last year."

"Do we have plans today, Dad?"

"Um, well, not really. Just to be together."

"Well, I could go over the names of the shells for you, but then sleep at Mom's. I have to unpack my new stuff and everything, anyway. Over at Mom's."

"Don't you want to stay here? I missed you. Why don't you stay here?"

"We could go over the shells and have a snack and Mom can wait in the car, or she can have a snack, too—"

"I made my famous chili and thought we could watch the game together."

"I don't care about the stupid game."

"Anna," they both said.

Then Dad said, "Go to your room."

I grabbed Mom around the waist. "I'll go to my room at Mom's."

"No, you'll go to your regular room here,"

he said.

"Nothing is regular here anymore. I hate it. I hate you!"

Mom started crying. (I know for sure I was the cause of that crying.)

There were a couple shells left on the floor. I stomped on them. It didn't do anything, so I let Moby roll out of my hand. He hit the tile and bounced a few times. And then I jumped right on him.

Hard.

He broke, and it made me cry more. It wasn't his fault about my parents and my dumb life. The stupid seashell didn't do anything wrong and I wrecked him anyway.

Dad escorted me to my room. That's what he said specifically, "I'm escorting you to your room, Anna. Let's go."

When we got there, I slammed the door in his face.

I thought for sure he'd come in after me.

I practically did a somersault to get into my closet behind the laundry basket.

But there was nothing but silence.

No one came in.

Downstairs, I could hear Mom and Dad, but it sounded like mumbling. And it went on for a long time that way, just mumbling, until the door shut, which meant Mom was gone.

An hour later....

I could hear the TV. It was March Madness when all the college teams get together and play each other every day in a row. I didn't know what kind of trouble I was going to be in for that "display," but I came out anyway. Dad was sleeping on the couch. I sat next to him.

"Oh, hi, honey."

"Hey, Dad."

He didn't seem to be mad anymore.

"Who's winning?"

"State was. Look at that, still winning. Up by twenty. Nice. Gotta hand it to their coach. He's the real deal."

"Do you...like the shells?" I felt nervous but asked anyway.

"I love 'em. Thank you, baby. I added them to my collection. Except for Bob. I glued him up good."

"Moby."

"Yes, Moby."

I smiled. Dad loved gluing stuff. Me, too. We had that in common, that and our long eyelashes and smelly feet. "Where is he, can I see him?"

"Well, Bob—I mean Moby—is in critical condition but stable. He's over on the counter—I mean in Room 303 of the South Wing of the Post-Surgical Unit. Visiting hours ended about fifteen minutes ago, but I'll make an exception for you. For family."

"Thanks, Dad," I giggled. "I mean Doctor."

I went into the kitchen to check on him. From far away he looked good. When I got close up, I couldn't believe Dad's big hands got all those tiny pieces glued back together.  I'd really busted him up good. I wanted to hold him, but he didn't look all the way dry, so I figured I better just say hi.

"Hi."

The Big Guy and the Little Guy were in their beds. I went over and pet their heads so they wouldn't be jealous of me talking to Bob—I mean Moby. After about a minute of dog talk with my voice real high, I went back to Room 303.

"I'm sorry about my violent outburst, Moby. It was childish and dramatic, and it won't happen again."

Well, now that I had that off my chest, you would have thought I would have felt better. But, no. I couldn't shake the feeling I had, even though I wanted to....

I went back into the living room.

"Dad. Do you think...."

"Do I think what, honey?" Dad asked 'cause I was stalling.

"Do you think I could sleep at Mom's? I really wanted to unpack and do stuff there before school starts. And, thank you for Moby. He looks just like brand new. Please?"

Dad stared at me for a minute or like three seconds. Then he tossed me his phone. "Go ahead."

Wow.

I couldn't believe it.

"Do you think I could take some of your

famous chili with me, for when I get hungry?"

"I already gave your mom a container."

Wow.

I couldn't believe it.

"Wonder woman has to eat, too, Anna. We can't let her go hungry. When she's not busy saving the world, she has to be in tiptop shape to be your mom."

Dad just said a nice thing about Mom—a really nice thing. And, he answered a question I didn't even ask, not out loud, anyway. I must have been thinking it so hard: *You gave Mom some of your favorite chili? Really?*

He'd started doing that lately: answering questions I was only thinking about in my head. He said it was because I had a terrible poker face. Whatever that meant.

On the walk to Mom's, I saw Grandma twinkling in the sky.

That was cool.

• • •

I didn't know it at the time, not exactly, but something Mom had called a breakthrough was happening.

That was the first of many nights I got to sleep at Mom's on Dad's night, but that's not what I meant by breakthrough, because I was starting to like it at Dad's. I just meant that my dumb and stupid life was feeling less dumb and stupid.

It's true that I was being forced to do all this stuff that mostly sucked and was embarrassing, too, like living in a cracker box with a bed in the living room pushed up against a (sky blue) brick wall, and wearing my gym teacher's weird, big sneakers, but other things were happening, too. Like, I was starting to see my parents like how I saw my friends: My parents were actual human people that had actual human feelings, and hopes and dreams and everything. And, sometimes they did stuff right, but sometimes they made mistakes like all the other humans on the planet.

I had never looked at my parents like two real human people before. I mean, my whole life—until now—there was Mom, and then there was Mom & Dad, a team. I guess that's how I saw it. Mom did all the mom stuff. That list is way too long to even make. Plus,

I'd probably only come up with 87 things, and then if Mom ever found the list she'd get hives 'cause a list with 87 things isn't a list. *"You need to have 75 or 100, Anna. This makes no sense! You're giving me hives!"* I could hear her in my head. But, I never really knew Dad all by himself. I just knew Mom & Dad together. And I sure didn't know they could be so happy and so sad, and sometimes be right and sometimes be wrong about stuff.

So, my dad, apparently, likes it when a person is calm. That's one of the things I never knew about him.

I could get my way with Dad if I was calm. That was the breakthrough I'd had on the couch that day with Bob in recovery and Michigan State beating the other guys by twenty. Dad escorted me to my room when I screamed and said I hated him. And, then, when I said please and was calm, he let me go to Mom's.

That breakthrough got me thinking: Crying must make Dad really mad for some reason, like a list with 19 things on it does with Mom. Maybe crying gives Dad hives...? Maybe that explains why he'd always ignored Mom when she cried. Maybe if he didn't ignore her, he'd yell and send Mom to her room, like he did with me. And that would make things—like his hives or their marriage—worse. Maybe ignoring her was his way of being calm or his way of being as nice as he could be, given the reality of the situation.

Maybe Mom never knew this.

Maybe she never got to have this kind of

breakthrough with Dad.

I should tell her!

If she knew that Dad could not handle the crying, that it made him crazy and uncomfortable like a list with 19 or 87 things on it, then maybe she'd give him a break for ignoring her.

What's the matter?

How'd you get so smart?

I spent so much time thinking about things like that now. All I really wanted to do was hula-hoop and hang with Sierra and wait for it to get warm, then Sierra and I could start chasing rainbows after the spring showers. And I could get a new bike like they had both promised.

With everything going on, would they even remember about the promise?

Those were the things I had to think about in my new life.

Mom was forgetting things left and right; that was the breakthrough I had had with her. I mentioned it to Dad, you know, mostly just to make conversation on the walk over to Mom's that night.

But Dad said, "Give her a break. She has a lot on her mind."

I rolled my eyes. *Yeah, we all have a lot on our mind....*

"We all have a lot on our mind, Anna."

Whoa.

And then together, we said, "Poker face!" and it was pretty funny.

After I unpacked at Mom's and got all snuggly under my covers, I felt a little bad about spending the whole vacation with Mom and not even one night with Dad.

There are certain things that Dad can do better than Mom. Chili was one of them. Staying calm was another. Dad was great at sports. You should see my mom shoot a basketball. On second thought, I hope you never have to witness that.

But my mom was still my mom. And, even if Dad glued all the Bobs in the world back together, he still wouldn't be Mom.

Moby. I mean Moby.

8

APRIL

Monday–Tuesday: Sleep at Mom's.

Wednesday–Thursday: Stay with Dad.

Friday–Sunday: Stay with Mom.

Monday–Tuesday: Sleep at Dad's.

Wednesday–Thursday: Stay with Mom.

Friday–Sunday: Threw a giant fit to be with Mom. Ended up at Dad's and in my room for a Time Out.

No TV Friday night; that's what he told me as he shut the door to my room. But that only lasted till 8:30 when Dad fell asleep and I switched from sports to my shows at 8:47. I asked him if it was okay and he mumbled, "Whatever you want, baby."

Woke up on Saturday and shot hoops with Dad, then took the dogs for a short walk, and then played fetch with the Little Guy. (The Big Guy was too lazy for fetch.) Then, we washed Dad's shadow black Ford F-150 until it sparkled like new even though it wasn't. Dad got it for a deal from one of his buddies. Later in the afternoon, I asked real sweet if I could stay with Mom. Dad tossed me his phone.

Saturday–Tuesday: Stayed with Mom.

Sunday night was tricky 'cause I had to

use Mom's phone to ask because it was still Dad's night. I couldn't twinkle my eyes with the long lashes and cuddle up to him. But I kept my cool and he finally said okay.

I stayed home from school on Tuesday. It was Mom's day.

You know how being nice and saying please a lot works for Dad? Well, having a fit and crying real loud works with Mom. I get a little more tired after that, but it's worth it to get my way.

So, Tuesday morning there was this spelling contest. It was for extra credit and I didn't want to do it. Even though I knew how to spell big words like specifically, reluctant, ridiculous, and rhetorical, I didn't want to stand up and talk in front of everyone. The last thing I needed was twenty-four tilted heads and sad smiles pointing in my direction and ruining my day. Twenty-five if I included my teacher. Anyway, I pitched a fit and got to watch my favorite shows with the volume over 30 and cereal with chocolate milk for breakfast.

And lunch.

With gummy bears for an in-between snack.

Talk about a win-win.

This gave me an opportunity to make my upcoming birthday list; that's what Mom said I could do with my spare time after I made the bed in the bedroom and rinsed out both my cereal bowls. I couldn't make the bed in the living room/bedroom 'cause I was snuggled up in it all day.

But I didn't need a birthday list. Like I said, I just wanted a bike.

Besides, lists weren't my thing anymore.

• • •

It felt so good and so easy to be home all day on Tuesday, that on Wednesday, I wanted to do it all over again. I knew there needed to be a real reason, though.

I planned it all out: I started by asking Mom for herbal tea for breakfast. She drank this a lot at night when she was curled up with a good book. And she'd always say, "Whoa, the herbal tea is making me so warm," and then she'd toss off the throw blanket that was across her legs. This was what gave me the idea. So, even though she looked at me funny when I requested it, she made it for me. I drank it real fast, then went and got into my school clothes. Then I came back out into the kitchen and said, "Mom, I really don't feel good. I think I'm getting the flu or something. You might want to take my temperature."

Mom said, "You think I was born yesterday, Anna? You think I don't know that a hot drink might make your mouth hotter and make you seem like you have a temperature?"

This was one of those times when I knew

it would be best to keep my eyes wide open and my mouth shut tight. Still, me being a kid and Mom being a mom....

"I feel sick and I don't want to go to school and you can't make me! I'm not going! I'm sick!"

"I know you're not sick. I gave you a freebie yesterday. You're going. Now get your shoes on. Please."

"They're probably not even here."

"I can see them—both of them—by the door."

"Because this house or apartment or whatever you call it is too small! That's why you can see my shoes from across all the rooms put together! It's built for hamsters! I hate it!"

"Anna, is something going on at school?

Are kids being mean to you?"

No one was being mean. They were all being nice and very careful, like when a baby is sleeping. It was all tippy toes and low talk at my school, like they were afraid to wake me.

I shook my head.

"Then put your shoes on or we're going to be late."

"No!" I screamed and ran into the bedroom and slammed the door.

Five minutes later....

Dad was at the door, dragging my butt to school.

Eight hours later....

Dad was in front of the school, dragging my butt into his shadow black Ford F-150.

Once I was buckled in tight, he gave me a

speech about advertising.[2] I don't think that's the right word. I got a speech about how bad things happen to everyone and how you handle it is the important part. He said he thought I was mostly doing a good job and he was proud of me, but then he added, "Your display this morning, Anna—you can't act like that. It's not okay to be disrespectful to your mom or me. You know you can talk to us."

He handed me a list of chores that was five things long. *I know who helped him make that list.*

It took two hours to unload the dishwasher, clean my bedroom, dust the

---

[2] adversity

whole entire house, take a nice walk with the Little Guy (the Big Guy was too lazy for long walks), and then sweep the kitchen. Dad said, "This'll give you time to think about your behavior." He was right about that.

Just as I was dumping the dust bunnies into the garbage can, there was a knock on the door.

"Hello? You guys home?"

"Mom?"

"Hi, honey."

Dad came into the kitchen from the living room just as Mom and Sierra walked in from outside.

"Hi…" I said to Sierra, basically ignoring Mom. I didn't mean to, I was just so surprised to see her.

"Hi…" Sierra said back.

Mom smiled. "We're only two blocks away, so when Sierra stopped by, I figured, why not walk her over."

"Sure," Dad said.

"I don't know if Anna's done with her list, but if she is, maybe they can play. If not, I can walk Sierra home."

"No, she's just finishing up. You hungry, Sierra?" Dad always asked everyone who came into the house if they were hungry.

"No, sir, I'm okay. Thank you."

"That's what I'm talking about. Respect." Dad arched an eyebrow at me.

I'd normally roll my eyes, but I was in shock. Frozen with a broom in one hand and a dustpan in the other. (That can happen for real, you know—freezing in one place from shock.)

"Well, why don't you girls go play," Mom said.

"Outside," Dad added. "Get outside and have some fun."

I looked from one to the other, then dropped the broom and dustpan and—

"Anna!" they yelled in stereo.

Then I picked up the broom and dustpan. I set them in the closet by the door, grabbed my hoodie, and left with Sierra.

We walked toward the park, one of our regular destinations, without talking for a little bit.

She finally said, "Wow, your parents don't seem like they're getting a divorce."

"Those aren't my parents. Those are aliens. I don't know what they did with my parents."

Sierra started laughing.

"And I had my suspicions but it's official now. I'm adopted."

Now Sierra was holding her belly and laughing.

"Do you think they used alien money to buy me? Is there such a thing as alien money? Or, maybe they scooped me up from my real parents' backyard, probably somewhere in Kansas. Weird stuff happens there."

"Anna, stop, I'm going to pee in my pants!" (She got that saying from her mom.) Sierra bent right over on the sidewalk with her legs crossed.

That's when I started laughing, too.

When we finally caught our breath, we started walking again. In silence again.

After another minute of that, Sierra said,

"I thought you didn't like me anymore."

"What?"

"You haven't called to color or watch a movie or to play H-O-R-S-E or anything."

"Because my life sucks, not because you're not my best friend."

She smiled a sad smile.

"And that's why! That smile. That's why I haven't called. I can't take any more tilted heads and sad smiles! The old Anna never got any sad smiles. Everyone was happy to see me. Now when people see me, I make them sad. And who wants to be the person that makes everyone sad? I don't want to be that person. I don't want this dumb life with my alien parents and two homes and nobody even looks at me like normal anymore!"

I stopped walking, turned, and headed

back toward the house. Not because I didn't want to be with Sierra, but I was going to cry real tears again and this was just the worst.

"Anna!"

I didn't want her to see me cry, but I also didn't want to be alone, not really, so I slowed down just a little bit. That's when I noticed it was sprinkling. Last year that would have made me so excited 'cause spring showers meant....

"Anna!" Sierra jumped in my path. Then she stared at me real funny, like she was noticing I had a nose for the first time. Then she exhaled the biggest breath right in my face. "I'm sad, too," she said, and her eyes got watery, but not from the tiny raindrops that were landing on her cheeks.

Then she blinked, and two tears popped

out of her eyes and left shiny tracks

all the way down to her chin.

I couldn't believe it.

I was pretty freaked out and didn't really know what to do, so I shrugged and tried to smile. "Sierra…." I didn't know what to say. I couldn't think of a single thing, so I hugged her.

She hugged me back.

When we were all done hugging like best friends do, she said, "You just did it, too."

"I did what?"

"You gave me a sad smile."

Whoa.

I think I did.

"And you tilted your head before you did it!"

Whoa.

I think I did.

"You know why you gave me a sad smile? Because I'm your best friend and that's what best friends do. They are sad together and happy together and that's how it's supposed to be with people that love each other."

I've always said Sierra should grow up to be the president and this was why.

I sighed like Mom and pulled it together like Dad said to do when things got "heavy."

The sprinkling had stopped.

"Do you still like to play H-O-R-S-E and make tulips?" she asked.

"Well, yeah." Duh.

"Do you still like to chase rainbows?"

"Yeah." Duh.

The sun was starting to peek through the clouds.

"Then that means the old Anna is the same as the new Anna."

"Yeah." I guess it did mean that.

"So, it doesn't matter if you have two homes or aliens for parents. You haven't changed at all. You're Anna either way."

"Yeah."

"Just like your—"

"My name!" I shouted.

See what I mean: Sierra for president.

The sun was all the way out from behind the darkest cloud in the sky.

Sierra and I looked up.

"Are you ready?" she asked.

I nodded.

And off we ran, chasing rainbows.

9

MAY

Dear Anna,

Happy Birthday, sweetheart. I am so proud of you. I love your laugh, your smile, your sweet face as it sleeps.

I love that you say "hi" to every baby you see, even if they're sleeping. I love that you make me take you to hold puppies at Pet Shop. And, I love that you are no longer begging me to take one home, that holding them is enough for you now.

Mostly, Anna, I love how much you love me. I don't take that for granted.

I didn't know all this before I gave birth to you. I didn't know I'd wind up with the best part of "me" living on the outside. This "best part of me" is smarter and funnier and tougher—and it's on the outside now. It's you! I am just so grateful to God for not only granting my wishes when he brought you to me but exceeding them beyond my imagination. I asked for a perfect daughter with big brown eyes and her grandmother's wit. I wanted her to be strong and happy and smart. I didn't ask that she be a lover of animals. I didn't ask God to make her verbose. But, you're all these incredible things, anyway: artist, athlete, storyteller—they all seem to be

140

your thing, Anna.

Thank you for pointing out the beautiful baby, the flower blooming between two cracks in the sidewalk, the rainbow in the sky after the spring showers. I can't count how many rainbows I would have missed if I hadn't given birth to you.

You are my favorite everything, Anna, my little palindrome.

I know this year has not been what you imagined. I know I can never fix that. Even if I could (fix it), I can't take back what has already happened. I hope you know I'm sorry. You have handled this year with great dignity. Your dad and I are amazed by you. And, yes, I will explain to you what "verbose" and "dignity" and some other words mean when you're done reading this. And, I know you've been sad, too. That part breaks my heart more than anything. I am sorry for every second of your sadness. I love you, sweetheart, with my heart, my head, my hands, my eyes, my soul, my breath.... I love you in my dreams.

Happy birthday.

Love,

Mom

I woke up to that (very long) letter from Mom. And I understood most of it. I understood that she was sorry. Dad was, too. I could tell by the look on his face every time he said hello, but specifically from how he said his goodbyes. He thinks he's good at hiding stuff, but he doesn't have the best poker face, either.

They both tried real hard to stay "normal" all year. It didn't work, but I could tell they tried. They also spent all the important days with me—I mean they spent them *together* with me. At the spring concert, sitting next to each other, that kind of stuff. I looked out from the stage at a sea full of sad head tilts, but not them! They were just sitting there, minding their own business, waiting for me and my class to sing. Their heads were normal, straight up and down. It was real weird at first—*them together but not together*—but then it became nice.

They took more pictures of me now in this new life we had, and they constantly sent them off to each other. I swear, no matter what I'd do, they'd take a photo. If I was eating a cheeseburger, it was caught on camera. This has gotten a little annoying, but it was also kind of cool. It was much better than no pictures. So, I smiled after I cut the grass at Dad's, and while I was hula hooping at Mom's in our living room/bedroom, or when I was holding my one hundredth puppy at Pet Shop, or playing with my little cousin, Buggie (whose house I was over at all the time now).

I'd smile again and again and again so one of them could send a picture of me to the other one. I smiled every day for them now.

It was my new thing.

This was not the way it used to be.

But it wasn't a whole lot worse, either.

I wasn't the only kid this has happened to: divorce. Of course, I didn't know that when it happened to me, but I sure knew it now.

I was the loneliest kid in the world last winter. But then one day, near the end of the school year, I realized that Becca had two houses, and Lucas had two houses, and so did Ian, and Jenna.

•••

It was almost summertime. There was usually only one month of school left after my birthday, and boy did that fly by every year. It was going even faster this year. You know why? Guess who got two bikes for their birthday? If you guessed "me," you were right! A mountain bike for Dad's and one that folds in half to fit at

Mom's!

Even Mom looked surprised when Dad came around the corner with the second bike.

She didn't look as surprised as me though....

Wow.

I couldn't believe it.

Then we had red velvet cake, which Mom made, and an ice cream cake, which Dad bought.

My aunt made a joke about Mom being "happy again" when she took a piece of each cake, the ice cream and the velvet. She used air quotes and slapped my mom on the butt after she said it.

Mom stuck out her tongue and said, "You're one to talk."

Sisters sure are weird.

10

SEPTEMBER

It's Tuesday, the first day of school. Summer was much better than I thought it would have been. At the Labor Day cookout, Mom said that was because summertime allows a person to regroup and rejuvenate. When I asked what the "R" words meant, Dad said, "What your mother means, Anna, is summertime allows people to ride their bikes and grill out." Well, I felt "regrouped" from all the bike riding and "rejuvenated" from all the hot dogs and freezy pops, that was for sure.

All the kids from last year who don't live in my neighborhood looked taller and extra smiley back at school. That's the first thing I noticed about being back. That included Sierra. Her family went traveling for a whole month in a giant camper, so I hadn't seen her in a while. Sierra's shiny, beautiful hair was two inches longer and she looked two inches taller, too. She was being pulled in all directions just like Grandpa said I was.

There were two new kids in my class, a boy and a girl. They were twins even though they looked nothing alike. *Those genes went together in a strange way*, I thought, but I

148

didn't say that out loud. One had really big front teeth; the other had none. One had blue eyes; the other had brown. But I kept all that information to myself, even though it seemed obvious. Their names were Max and Hannah. Also, super weird. I would have thought Max and Jax, or Hannah and…huh? Nothing really rhymes with Hannah that would be a good name for a boy twin.

But Hannah was a palindrome!

I couldn't wait to tell her. I thought of it as a sign that we should be friends.

Today was turning out to be really great. And, I hadn't gotten a single head tilt, even when I ran into the gym teacher. Everyone's been asking "how's your mom?" and I've been answering "great!" and no one's tilted anything.

But, then, during third period, I asked to go to the bathroom, and that's when I found out about Malina. She was going to have two houses.

Malina was crying in a stall, so I asked (naturally), "What's the matter?"

That's when she told me about her parents separating and she said that her dad was moving to the town that's one town over from ours.

Last year, I wouldn't have known what to say....

"It's okay, Malina, I have two houses, too. Sometimes it's fun. I have a bike at one, and a scooter *and a bike* at the other, and I get to pick out my favorite cereal at the grocery store all the time now. Sometimes, I even eat it with chocolate milk. And I smile a lot for pictures. Wait till they make you start smiling a lot for pictures. It's annoying at first, but then it gets fun. Oh, and maybe you'll even get to go to Pet Shop and hold puppies every week. That part is the best."

She stopped crying and looked up at me. Most kids my age look up at me 'cause I'm so tall. Then she smiled. "Do you think my mom will let me take home one of those puppies?"

"I don't know. Is your mom a pushover?"

"What's that?"

"I'll tell you on the way to class."

We walked back to class, arm in arm. I explained what a pushover was and how one parent, usually the mom, will probably turn into one—a real pushover—when she gets two houses, at least for a little while. "And that's when you can use tactics to get your way," I told her. Then I explained that I'd explain what "tactics" were at lunch because your brain needs time to process new stuff.

Malina's eyes got real wide. Then she smiled again.

There are some perks to my new life. Not the bike and scooter or the chocolatey cereal (which is cool), but I'm talking about making Malina smile. I'm glad for that.

When we got back to class, Malina stopped outside the door. "Can you tell that I've been crying?"

Her eyes had just a couple of tiny, red splotches under them. "No," I said. "You look perfect." Mom always said that to me after I was crying. I'm pretty sure it doesn't count as a fib.

Malina smiled again, a third time, which made me smile. Again.

Just as we were going in, our new teacher, came out. "Malina, please find your seat. Anna, I need to speak with you."

Uh-oh.

"Sweetheart, you need to grab your bag. Your mom is at the hospital. Your dad will be here in ten minutes to get you."

"But—"

"It's okay, Anna. Your dad said to tell you everything is okay. You don't have to worry. You were two weeks early, too, and look how perfect you are."

"Did he say that?"

"Yes, actually, he did. He said to tell you that exactly. He must know you pretty well," she added and tapped my nose.

"He does. My dad knows me really well," I said, because, well, he did. He knew my favorite TV show now, and my favorite toothpaste—which was none! He knew I was good at drawing tulips but not puppies. He knew I could get cranky in the morning time if I went to bed after eight forty-five the night before. And he was starting to catch onto my different smiles, like, the regular one and the one I use when I try to get my way. He said he could spot that one a mile away, the sneaky one. He told me I had to get new material. Whatever that meant.

I knew him, too. I knew if he was quiet that meant he was mad or sad. Loud was always happy. Watching sports was important to him, and so was keeping his truck nice. And, I knew that my sneaky smile would always work on him, even though he'd caught onto it.

I went and grabbed my backpack and stood looking out the window of the entrance doors, watching for Dad's shiny and clean shadow black Ford F-150.

The sun was big in the sky. Everything was a super-duper shade of green. I thought about how nothing looked the same as last year, even though those were still the same silver maple trees—all lined up one, two, three, four, five in front of the school. I would wait by tree number five for Mom just like last year, except only on her days now. And when fall came, I would watch for the spinners—the seeds that look like helicopters—and I would try to catch them on their way down, just like I did last year.

It's just exactly the same sun in the sky. I bet it was even shining on this same day last year.

But it all feels different.

Mom said I couldn't have a list that was 19 things long. She even said I couldn't have a list that was 4 things long when I sacrificed practically the whole list for Dad. But she was wrong. I gave up the part of the list that had "Baby Brother" on it so that Dad would come home, but I guess it didn't matter. My list still worked in its own way. This was one of those things that you couldn't explain. Mom called it a miracle. Santa was really late with this present and I wanted to be mad about that, but Mom said he wasn't late. She told me that sometimes presents come on time, but you have to wait to open them.

This year I got two bikes, a scooter, and some socks, and, well, I wanted everyone in the same house, but I didn't get that. Or the puppies. But miracles, like Mom said, have happened, and I was about to get one of the things on the Christmas list that I had given up.

And, I haven't seen Mom cry, not once, not the whole summer.

"We will make it work with the two houses," Dad said that to her just last week when she walked me over. Then he told her not to worry because if it wasn't this, it would be something else. "When moms and dads aren't together anymore, life can get pretty interesting. Right, Anna?"

"That's a rhetorical question. Right, Dad?"

"How'd you get so smart?"

I looked up at Mom. She was, after all, the main reason I knew all the big words.

Then she said, "She must have gotten it from her father along with those eyelashes and smelly feet."

Wow.

I couldn't believe it.

And then we all smiled.

I didn't get that feeling like my parents would get back together when they were nice to each other now; I just felt normal.

Feeling normal was pretty cool.

• • •

My baby brother, Neven, was born at 2:29 p.m. on the first day of the new school year.

After Dad picked me up, he went through a drive-thru, which hardly ever happened, but we were in a rush. We got our sandwiches but then they told us to pull up for the fries. Well, Dad pulled up and waited for almost a whole minute, but then he peeled out—it made the coolest screeching sound—and went straight to the hospital. He wanted to get there for the baby. He wanted me to eat, too, but he said I'd be okay with the sandwich and the strawberry shake. It was only eleven in the morning and we could worry about more food later. He also said the baby wasn't going to be on our schedule; we were going to be on his and we might as well get used to it.

I waited in the special area where there were magazines, a TV, games, and a box of toys for the little, little kids. My aunt who doesn't speak Chinese was with me. We played checkers (not Chinese checkers, of course).

Then, at three o'clock on the nose, they called us in. Just when all my friends were getting out of their first day of school and catching the bus or walking home under the big sun or waiting for their moms under the silver maple trees, I was holding baby Neven in my arms.

I couldn't wait to draw him his first picture and introduce him to the Big Guy and the Little Guy and explain how Dad named the dogs. And then I'll tell him not to worry because Dad does this; he comes up with crazy names and then they grow on you. And then baby Neven will ask me what that means: "to grow on you." And then I'll get to start explaining stuff, just like Mom!

I couldn't wait to take him to Pet Shop to hold the little puppies. I couldn't wait to show him my rock collection and introduce him to the only seashell in the history of the world to ever be named Bob. And I really couldn't wait to point to the shiniest star in the sky and explain about our other grandma.

Oh, in case you were wondering, I picked out my baby brother's name. It was another one of the perks of my new life. I got to make big decisions sometimes. Naming Neven was one of those times.

When I get home tonight, after drawing him a picture, I'm going to make a list of all the things we're going to do together. I think I'll make it 93 things long.

I am still Anna, after all.

Welcome
to the
world,
NEVEN

LOVE,
ANNA

ANNA EITHER WAY